THE ADVENTUROUS SQUIRRELS OF COOL WATERS COVE

BY STEVEN WHYSEL

ILLUSTRATED BY QUINN CHAVEZ

LUMINARE PRESS

WWW.LUMINAREPRESS.COM

TO MY WIFE WENDY MY IRRESISTIBLE MUSE,
RICK BANKS FOR HIS WISE EDITING AND
TO THE TOP NOTCH CREW AT LUMINARE PRESS
WHO MADE MY SQUIRRELS' SHINE

CHAPTER 1
GETTING READY

In a big forest village called Happy Land U.S.A., inside a giant oak tree lived a family of famous adventurous squirrels.

Sir Daddyhad and Sweet Peanuts raised two wonderful little girl squirrels. Big sister, Gems, had the curliest tail you have ever seen, and her sister Pie had the tiniest nose. Excitement bubbled from each of them when they joined the most famous animal circus in the world, Poppy's Amazing Animal Circus.

3

Tomorrow is the first day of the big show, so today the squirrel family would soon practice their tricks, falls, slips and flips, and their amazing squirrels on the high wire act. Before they went out to practice, they had to have breakfast. They asked their mommy to make their favorite. She called it the Forest Breakfast Special. It contained acorns, walnuts, and a special nut that is very hard to find. This tasty nut, shaped like a little chicken egg, was called an egg nut.

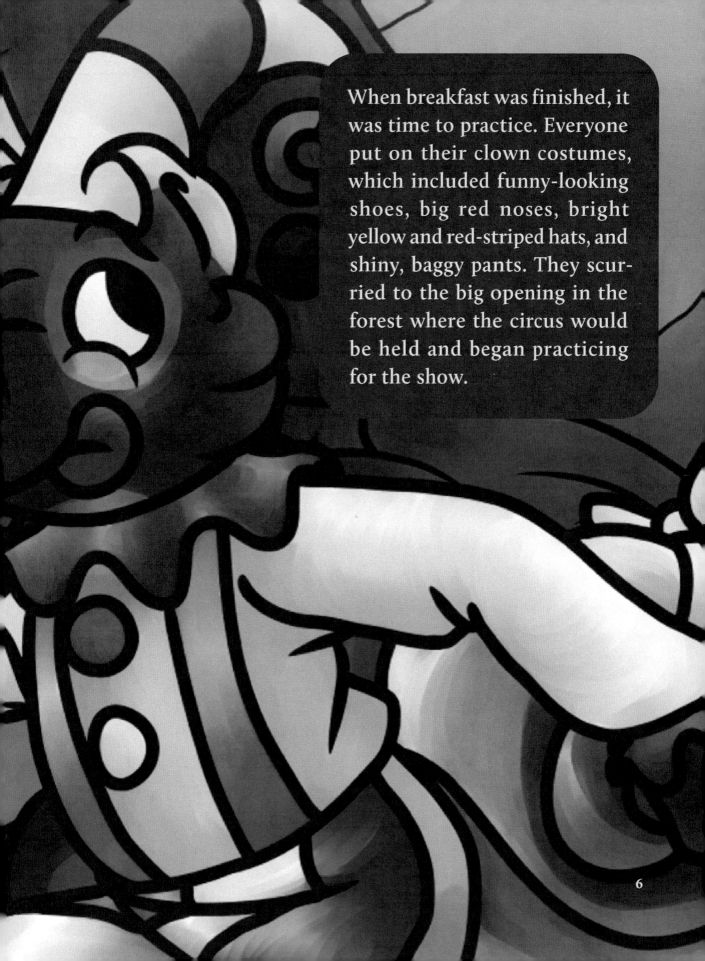

When breakfast was finished, it was time to practice. Everyone put on their clown costumes, which included funny-looking shoes, big red noses, bright yellow and red-striped hats, and shiny, baggy pants. They scurried to the big opening in the forest where the circus would be held and began practicing for the show.

6

Sir Daddyhad brought his fake banana and threw it on the ground. Then the girls slipped on the make-believe banana skin and fell with loud thumps. They had planned wisely that morning when they got dressed. They put fluffy pillows in their underpants.

The next trick was called the Magic Balloon Trick. Sweet Peanuts put water in a balloon, and Gems and Pie played catch. Then Gems threw the balloon over Pie's head into a group of watching animals and when a little monkey caught it, it burst open and out came lots of paper sprinkles. Oh, what a surprise! Everybody laughed loudly. Only the squirrels knew how they were able to change the water to paper sprinkles.

The family loved to ride around the circus ring on a special bicycle with four seats, throwing little furry toy squirrels to the young animals watching around the ring. Next, they go into the audience and put big red noses on the monkeys, rabbits, and other animals.

Finally, the squirrel family practiced their most famous trick, the High Wire Act. Soon you will know how this amazing trick is done and oh boy, you will be surprised!

The next day would be the first day of the real circus. So off they went to eat dinner, get a good night's sleep, and have sweet dreams about all the fun they would have tomorrow.

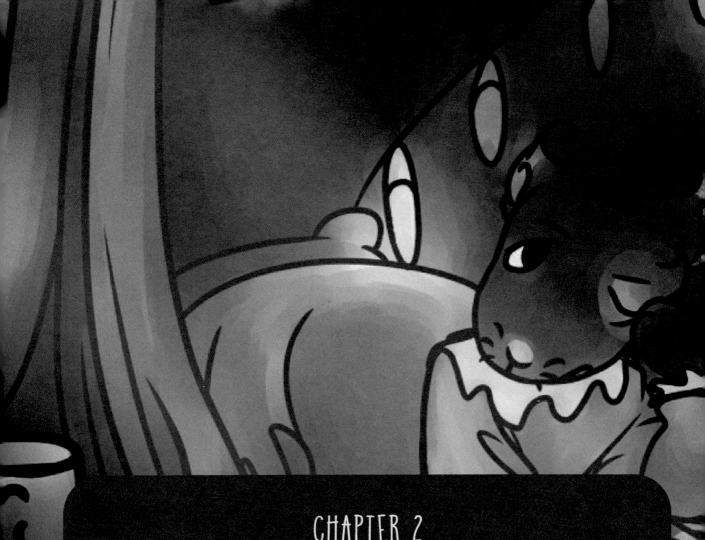

CHAPTER 2
THE BIG DAY

Gems was the first one to get out of her straw bed early that morning. Her excitement made it difficult to sleep. She climbed up the ladder that went from their home deep inside the big oak tree to the opening in the tree trunk. There she could see the sun just peeking out. She hurried back down to Pie's bedroom and tapped Pie on her paw to wake her.

Pie jumped up and asked, "Why did you wake me so early? I was having such a great dream!"

Gems asked her what her dream was about, and Pie said, "I was at a birthday party eating a great big piece of nut cake that was made of acorns, chestnuts, and the sweetest berries I have ever eaten. I want to go back to my dream. Leave me alone!"

Gems asked, "did you forget what day this is? We need to get ready for opening day at the circus! Let's get dressed in our costumes and then wake Mommy and Daddy."

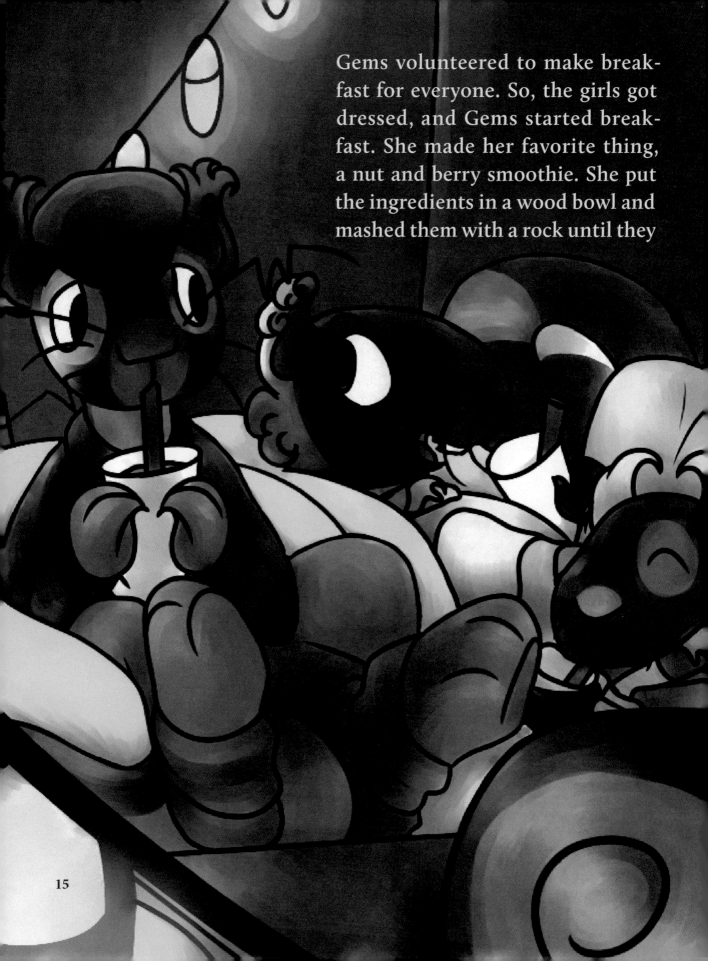

Gems volunteered to make breakfast for everyone. So, the girls got
dressed, and Gems started breakfast. She made her favorite thing,
a nut and berry smoothie. She put
the ingredients in a wood bowl and
mashed them with a rock until they

15

looked like pudding. By that time Mommy and Daddy were dressed. Everyone ate with excitement and thanked Gems for such a special treat.

Then they jumped onto their special bicycle-built-for-four and peddled to the big opening in the forest where the circus would soon begin. Families of rabbits, monkeys, squirrels, chipmunks, deer, raccoons, and bears took their seats in the trees and on the rocks, logs, and grass all around the show ring.

The clowns and acrobats started the show. Out came a big black bear wearing a bright red hat and striped red pants. He stood in the middle of the show ring and announced: "Welcome all you little and big forest animals to the biggest and best animal circus on earth, POPPY'S AMAZING ANIMAL CIRCUS. Now let the show begin!"

First came the jumping deer with cute monkeys standing on their backs waving flags. The monkeys wore bright yellow costumes with pointed hats and spinners on top.

The next act was the dancing raccoons. They stood in a circle and shook their tails. Then they sat on their back paws and wiggled their noses to say goodbye.

The animals watching went wild with squeaks, chirps, snorts, and whistles.

Now it was time for the Adventurous Circus Squirrels to perform. They started with all the tricks they rehearsed the day before, and now they were ready for their High Wire Act. ARE YOU READY TO BE SURPRISED? A wire was tied high above the ground between two tall trees. First, Sir Daddy had climbed up one tree and stood on the wire balancing on his two back paws. Next, Sweet Peanuts climbed up that tree, jumped, and sat on Sir Daddyhad's shoulders. Then Gems climbed all the way to her mommy's shoulders and sat down. Finally, little Pie very, very, slowly crawled all the way up and sat on Gems' shoulders. Sir Daddyhad's legs were shaking a little, but he did not lose his balance.

They were all a little shaky but didn't fall, so Sir Dad-dyhad started to VERY, VERY slowly inch-by-inch walk across the wire. All the animals watched with their eyes and mouths wide open, and many held their breath. When the squirrels reached the other tree, all of the animals let out yells and whistles. The family climbed down to the ground carefully, smiling and bowing to everyone.

The circus was now over, and all of the animals clapped their front paws and cheered loudly. Everyone went home happy with great big smiles.

THE END

Made in United States
Orlando, FL
27 June 2023

34592137R00020